THE GOOD SPORTS LEAGUE #2

THE PERFECT PITCH

By **TOMMY GREENWALD**

Illustrated by **LESLEY VAMOS**

AMULET BOOKS • NEW YORK

Cataloging-in-Publication Data has been applied for and may be obtained from the Library of Congress.

ISBN 978-1-4197-6367-0

Text © 2023 Tommy Greenwald
Illustrations © 2023 Lesley Vamos
Book design by Chelsea Hunter and Brann Garvey

Printed and bound in U.S.A.
10 9 8 7 6 5 4 3 2 1

Amulet Books are available at special discounts when purchased in quantity for premiums and promotions as well as fundraising or educational use. Special editions can also be created to specification. For details, contact specialsales@abramsbooks.com or the address below.

ABRAMS The Art of Books
195 Broadway, New York, NY 10007
abramsbooks.com

To Alicia Keys,
musician who ran a marathon;
to Justin Tucker,
placekicker and opera singer;
to Tina Fey,
high school actor, journalist, and tennis player;
and to everyone who finds joy in many things.
"Variety is the spice of life."

PROLOGUE

During the softball season, Annabella Donatello and her manager, Coach Grandy, had developed a routine.

Before the first inning of every game Annabella pitched, they would stand next to each other just outside the dugout, and Coach Grandy would look Annabella in the eye.

"Perfect day, perfect game, perfect pitch," the coach would say. Then she would hold out the ball. "Now go out there and get 'em."

Annabella would take the ball and say, "Perfectly happy to do so!"

This routine was their good luck charm, and one thing was for sure—it was definitely working.

Annabella Donatello had become the best pitcher in the league.

Hello, good friends! Frederick Ulysses Nimbleshank here, although my closest friends (like you) call me Freddy!

We're here at the West Harbor Softball Complex, where the West Harbor Smashers and the Portsmouth Seasiders are locked in a 1–1 tie.

Manager Jennifer Grandy's Smashers lineup has been quiet, but luckily, her two star pitchers, Annabella Donatello and Sadie Lederman, have been on fire.

Annabella pitched the first three innings and was lights out, striking out seven Seasiders;

Sadie has pitched the last three, only giving up a single run.

CHAPTER ONE
THE EVERYTHING GIRL

Annabella Donatello's mom sometimes called her daughter the "Everything Girl," because Annabella liked to do everything.

She liked to draw, she liked flying kites, she liked playing soccer for the Green Peppers in the Pizza League, she liked cooking, and she liked eating what she cooked.

She even liked doing math.

MATH?!?!

One day Annabella was watching television, and she saw a person juggling oranges.

"I want to try that," Annabella said.

"Please don't," her mom said. "It takes weeks to learn how to juggle, and in the meantime, I'll be scraping oranges off the wall."

Annabella learned how to juggle in four days, two hours, and forty-seven minutes, and no smushed oranges had to be scraped off any walls, which was a good thing, because Ms. Donatello was already a single mom who worked two jobs.

One of her jobs was the adoption coordinator at the West Harbor Animal Rescue Center. Annabella volunteered there whenever she could, because she loved dogs. Her favorite was Scruffy, an older mixed breed who came to the shelter missing one eye and half her hair. Scruffy was very sweet and playful but had yet to be adopted. Annabella loved playing with Scruffy.

She loved the cage-cleaning part less.

But of all the activities Annabella Donatello enjoyed, there were two that she loved most of all.

The first was softball.

Annabella started playing softball as soon as she could walk. She was a dominant pitcher, a superb fielder, and could hit the ball all the way to the next town.

The second thing Annabella loved more than anything was performing. She always seemed to be onstage: putting on plays for her mom, singing in the shower, telling stories at lunch.

"Do you think I could make it to Broadway one day?" she asked the school music teacher, Mr. Ketchnik.

Mr. Ketchnik thought for a moment, then said, "I think your passion and energy can take you as far as you want to go."

"Thanks!" said Annabella, before adding, "I think."

When Annabella was able to combine her two favorite things—softball and performing—it was the best thing of all!

So it was no wonder that after the big win against the Portsmouth Seasiders, when the team did their postgame chant, Annabella could be heard above everyone else.

We're the Bashers!

We're the Slashers!

We're the Mashers!

But mostly . . . we're the Smashers!

Gooooooooooo SMASHERS!

Sadie Lederman, who was so serious about softball that she wore eye black under her eyes even when it wasn't sunny, glared at Annabella. "Do you always have to sing so loud?"

"YEEESSS!" sang Annabella, in her loudest voice.

Coach Grandy clapped her hands together. "Solid win out there today, girls. You fought really hard. But to be honest, the hitting wasn't great. In fact, it was the opposite of great. So even though we have a game tomorrow afternoon, we're going to have an extra batting practice in the morning at ten a.m."

All the girls nodded, except for one.

Annabella.

Instead, she raised her hand. "Excuse me, Coach? As much as I would love to go to this last-minute-unscheduled-not-on-the-calendar practice, I have my friend Jay-Jay's birthday party."

"Hey, wait a second," said Sadie. "I'm going to the party too, but it's not till eleven."

Annabella glared at Sadie. "Right, the party is at eleven, but Trini and I have to go to the mall to buy Jay-Jay's present first."

"Why do you always wait until the last minute?" Sadie asked.

"Why do you never mind your own business?" Annabella asked in return.

"You two, hush!" said Coach Grandy. "So, Annabella, you're saying you are unable to attend this practice?"

Annabella shook her head. "I'm sorry, I promised Trini," she said.

The coach did not look happy. "Yes, well speaking of promises, you also promised your full commitment to this program and this team, did you not?"

Annabella's ears started to burn. "I swear I'll be at pre-game warmups right on time!"

"Well, aren't we all so grateful for that," said Coach Grandy, with a sarcastic edge to her voice. As soon as she turned to gather up the equipment, Sadie wrinkled her nose at Annabella.

Annabella almost wrinkled her nose back but then decided not to.

She stuck out her tongue instead.

CHAPTER TWO

QUESTION: IS CAKE GOOD FOR YOU?

Who doesn't love a magic show, am I right???
Hi again, folks. Freddy here with some
nonstop birthday party action!

We're celebrating the tenth birthday of Jay-Jay Wright,
one of the town's fine young citizens, and the main
attraction is . . .

Marvelous Marvin,
Master of Magic!

"How the heck did he do that?!?" Trini Tellez asked Annabella. Their eyes were as wide as the Grand Canyon.

"I have no idea," said Annabella. "And where's Jay-Jay?"

All the kids started murmuring as they realized Jay-Jay was nowhere to be found. Suddenly, Ben Cutler pointed up at a tree and cried out, "WHOA, NO WAY!" There was Jay-Jay, waving down at his friends.

"Here I am!" he shouted, excitedly.

The crowd is going **BONKERS**

After the show—which included another marvelously mysterious trick in which a large bowl of cherries somehow turned into a rooster—everyone crowded around Jay-Jay. The kids were hoping for some explanation about how he went from being inside a crate to up in a tree, but he refused to spill the beans. "A magician's assistant never tells," he explained, as Marvelous Marvin and his rabbit took selfies with their adoring fans.

Then Jay-Jay's mom rang a loud bell. "TIME FOR CAKE!" she hollered.

The kids started stampeding toward a long picnic table. In the middle of the table sat a ginormous, glorious-looking chocolate cake, its icing glistening in the sun.

Annabella's stomach started to grumble in the best way, and she was about to follow the herd when she felt a tap on her shoulder.

"Are you having cake?" asked Sadie Lederman.

"Of course I am," answered Annabella. "Why?"

Sadie looked disappointed that Annabella even had to

ask. "Because we have a big game later, that's why. All the sugar and calories and stuff will make you tired."

"But I love sugar and calories and stuff."

"Fine." Sadie shook her head sadly. "But when you can't make it all the way around the bases, don't come crying to me."

"Okay, Sadie. Good to know."

"What was that about?" Trini asked.

"Sadie is getting on my nerves," Annabella said.

"Uh-oh," Trini said, giggling just a tiny bit.

"Yesterday she gave me a hard time when I said I had to miss practice this morning, and just now she gave me a hard time for eating cake on game day."

"Oh, well I get that. Eating cake on game day is a terrible idea."

Annabella eyed her best friend. "Wait, are you serious? Are you not having cake? I know you have dance class later."

Trini was a fantastic dancer, and she took dancing as seriously as Sadie took softball.

"Probably not," Trini said. Then she grinned. "Meaning, I'm PROBABLY NOT going to tell my dance instructor that I had a piece."

Annabella giggled. "I'm PROBABLY NOT going to tell my coach either."

"Race you over there!" cried Trini.

"Go!" cried Annabella.

Annabella beat Trini to the cake line easily because she was the fastest girl in school, but there were already two kids ahead of her.

Luckily, she was still able to get one of the corners with the most icing.

CHAPTER THREE

ANSWER: AS IT TURNS OUT, YES!

"Perfect day, perfect game, perfect pitch," Coach Grandy said. "Now go out there and get 'em."

"Perfectly happy to do so!" Annabella said back.

Then she took the mound and went to work.

> Well, it was supposed to be a battle between the two best teams in the league, but so far, it's been pretty one-sided . . . West Harbor is way out in front, leading North Harbor 5–0. Things are well in hand, and the Smashers seem set to take sole possession of first place . . .

> Annabella Donatello pitched the first three innings, and now Sadie Lederman takes over for the fourth . . .

Annabella watched the ball fly over the fence, and she couldn't believe it. Sadie was almost as good a pitcher as she was! What was happening?

Coach Grandy walked to the mound again, this time to take Sadie out of the game. Annabella ran in from short-stop. "Don't worry about it, Sadie! We got this!"

But Sadie didn't look at her or say anything. Instead, she just handed the ball to the coach and trudged off the field.

Now we're in the bottom of the sixth and last inning, with West Harbor up to bat, the score tied 7–7 . . .

Annabella Donatello works out a walk . . . Selma Menzo comes to bat . . .

We're the Bashers!

We're the Slashers!

We're the Mashers!

But mostly . . . we're the Smashers!

Gooooooooooo SMASHERS!

As the team jumped up and down chanting and celebrating, Annabella saw her mom waving from the parking lot. Even though Ms. Donatello worked almost all the time and couldn't go to many of Annabella's games, she was always there for a ride when her daughter needed one.

Annabella pulled herself out of the pile and walked over to Coach Grandy.

"Way to beat the throw home," said the coach. "Really smart baserunning."

"Thanks, Coach Grandy," said Annabella. "How's Sadie doing?"

"Oh, she'll be okay. It's one bad game, no big deal. She'll bounce back just fine."

"I sure hope so," Annabella said. She snuck another peek at her mom. "Um, Coach, is it okay if I go?"

Coach Grandy frowned. "We haven't done our postgame stretching yet or handed out next week's schedule."

"Right, I know, and I'm so sorry. It's just that I have tryouts for the school play tomorrow and I really need to start practicing."

"You're trying out for the school play?"

"Yup, we're doing *The Lion King*. I'm hoping to play Scar."

"Scar?"

"He's the mean lion."

"I know who Scar is." Coach Grandy took her hat off and scratched her head. "Why are you always in such a rush, Annabella?"

Annabella smiled happily. "I just like doing lots of stuff, I guess."

The coach smiled back less happily. "There seems to be a pattern developing here, Annabella. A pattern of you having other priorities that get in the way of the team. I'm getting increasingly concerned."

"You don't have to be, I swear!" insisted Annabella. "Softball is my total priority! I love it!"

"But you love other things too, it appears." Coach Grandy sighed. "Do I have your word that this school play won't get in the way of your commitment to this team?"

"Oh, you do, and it won't!"

"Fine. Go on, then."

The last thing Annabella heard before getting in her mom's car was Sadie Lederman saying, "Where's she going *now*?"

CHAPTER FOUR

WATCH OUT FOR THAT TUBA!

"Very nice," said Mr. Ketchnik.

Annabella beamed. "Thanks! Did I make the show?"

"We'll announce the cast tomorrow."

"I really hope I can be Scar!"

Mr. Ketchnik raised his bushy eyebrows. "Ah, yes. A wonderful part. We shall see."

"I can't wait!"

As Annabella waited for her mom to pick her up, she thought about all the great things that had happened. She'd won two softball games, gone to a party and had chocolate cake, and hopefully-probably-almost-definitely made the school play.

It was more than a perfect day.

It was *two* perfect days!

CHAPTER FIVE
A WALK AND A TALK

Pitching was great.

Hitting home runs was the best.

Singing was amazing.

But of all the things Annabella liked to do, there was one simple activity that made her feel more relaxed than any other.

Taking Scruffy for a walk at the shelter.

Which is exactly what Annabella was doing when her mom came out from the office, waving her phone in the air.

"You got it!" she yelled. "You got it!"

Annabella was confused. "I got what?"

"ROOOAAARRRR!" roared her mom, and suddenly Annabella understood.

"I got Scar? NO WAY!"

"WAY!"

Annabella and her mother screamed so loudly that Scruffy nearly jumped out of her furry skin.

"Oh no!" Annabella said, rubbing Scruffy's ear. "I'm sorry I scared you, Scruff!"

Ms. Donatello put her hand on her daughter's shoulder. "I'm so proud of you, honey. You deserve this."

They hugged, and then her mom put her arms around her daughter and looked her in the eye. "You're sure you can handle all this, right hon?"

"What do you mean, Ma?"

"I mean, you're a very busy girl, and the playoffs are coming up, and I don't want you to bite off more than you can chew."

Annabella pointed at Scruffy, who was busy chomping on a large stick. "You mean, like her?"

Annabella's mother laughed. "You know what I mean."

"If this is about driving me around and picking me up

all the time, I totally get it," Annabella said. "I can start biking more, and looking for carpools—"

"It's not that, honey, I promise. It's just that I know how much you love softball, and how much you love singing and performing, and you're already talking about maybe joining the travel soccer team next year, and I think it's awesome, I really do, as long as it's not too much."

"Too much? Jeez, Ma, I'm only ten!"

"I know. But these days, even being ten can be stressful."

"Not to me! I got this, trust me."

Ms. Donatello hugged her daughter. "Okay, Annabean. I trust you."

Annabella got a warm feeling in her heart. Annabean had been her nickname since she was a baby. She loved it when her mom called her that. It made her feel special.

"Can I give Scruffy a snack?" she asked.

Her mom winked. "I may have a few extra biscuits at my desk."

As Annabella took Scruffy inside for a treat, she felt like the luckiest girl in the world.

The busiest, but also the luckiest.

CHAPTER SIX
NOW PITCHING FOR THE SMASHERS . . . A LION?!

For the next few weeks, what Annabella told her mom was totally true; she was able to live her very busy life, even as the softball season got more intense. Coach Grandy was understanding about her schedule, but that might have been because Annabella was the team's best hitter and best pitcher.

Mr. Ketchnik, meanwhile, was very excited that he had a superstar athlete in his cast. One day, Annabella ran into rehearsal with a big grass stain on her softball pants, still out of breath.

"Exciting game today?" asked Mr. Ketchnik.

"That's for sure," she panted. "And it just ended twelve minutes ago."

"Well, I'm glad you enjoy sports, because they can help us in our own training," Mr. Ketchnik said. "For example, as you are huffing and puffing so heavily, this would be a good day to work on our breathing technique. Every performer must realize how important it is to stay calm and settle down. So let's start with some deep breathing exercises." Mr. Ketchnik lowered his voice to a whisper. "Everyone, picture an ocean . . . the waves going in and out . . . crashing onto the shore . . . now time your breaths to those waves . . . in . . . out . . ."

For the next ten minutes, as the entire cast of *The Lion King* breathed in and out, Annabella felt herself relax.

"Thanks, Mr. Ketchnik!" she said.

Three days later, the West Harbor Smashers were playing in their first playoff game, against Bernville Elite Softball. Annabella was pitching a shutout, but in the fifth inning, a Bernville batter hit a home run to make the score 6–1. Annabella glared at the ball as it went over the fence, then started pacing around the mound and growling.

Coach Grandy went out to the mound, and Sadie Lederman ran in from shortstop.

Annabella was staring straight ahead. "*I answer to no one,*" she said in an abnormally low voice.

The coach looked concerned. "Annabella? Are you okay?"

Annabella looked like she was in a trance. "I am Scar," she said.

"Who?" asked Sadie.

"I am Scar the lion," Annabella said, "and I am displeased."

Sadie's eyes widened in disbelief. "Uh, are you serious right now? This is a playoff game! If we lose, we're out!"

Sadie turned to Coach Grandy. "Do you want me to pitch, Coach? I can take over!"

But Annabella shook her head. *"I answer to no one.* Scar says that in *The Lion King*. The new one, actually, even though we're doing a version closer to the animated movie in school."

Coach Grandy looked at Annabella carefully. "Well, Scar, let's see what you've got. Go ahead and do what you have to do."

Annabella laughed in what could only be described as a lionlike way. "I shall indeed, Coach. I shall indeed."

She struck out the next three batters on nine pitches, and on her way back to her dugout, she glared at the Bernville bench.

"Life's not fair, is it?" she growled.

CHAPTER SEVEN

RACE AROUND THE BASES

Hey gang, let's hear it for every kid's favorite time of day . . .

RECESSSSSSSSSSS!!!!!

We've got something serious going on today . . . a kickball game between Ms. Farkle's class against Mr. Blintzer's that's getting super intense.

Lucas McGoish is on the mound for the Farkles, and he's been going with his fancy schmancy Swirler-Bouncer pitch, which is fooling the Blintzers big time. They keep popping it up right and left . . .

but uh-oh, here comes Annabella Donatello up to bat . . . or up to kick . . .

The Farkles ended up winning 22–19, but that didn't make Lucas feel much better. He was considered by everyone to be the best athlete in the grade, and he didn't like to be shown up by anyone. Especially in front of the whole school.

So something had to be done about that.

"Hey, Anna Banana," he said, as the two teams left the field.

Annabella stopped gabbing with her friends and turned around. "My name is Annabella."

"Okay, fine then—*Annabella*. I, uh, just wanted to say that was a pretty good kick. For a girl."

"Actually, I thought it was a pretty good kick for anyone," said Annabella. "But thank you just the same . . . McGoish Banoish."

Everyone giggled, which made Lucas's face turn red.

"Wanna race?" he blurted out.

"Race?" Annabella scrunched up her face in confusion. "Like, a running race? Now?"

"Yeah, why not?"

"Because recess is over in two minutes, that's why not."

Lucas dropped the big red rubber ball he was holding. "C'mon. One time around the bases. It'll take thirty seconds."

Annabella sighed. She wasn't really in the mood to race an irritating boy, but everyone was watching and she didn't see a way out of it. "Okay, fine," she said. "Although I'm not sure how losing to me in a race will make you feel better."

"Hahaha, very funny!" Lucas clapped his hands together. "Cool! Let's do this."

Whoa, lookie here! Just when you thought it was time to head back inside to books and learning and stuff, we've got ourselves a surprise extra-credit treat—a race between Lucas McGoish and Annabella Donatello, the two best athletes in the grade. Looks like they're going to do a dash around the bases for all the marbles . . .

"Who won???" gasped a totally out-of-breath Lucas McGoish. "I got her at the end, right?"

But no one was really paying attention to Lucas. Instead, everyone ran to Annabella, who was holding her shoulder. Trini was the first to reach her.

"Are you okay?" Trini asked. "What happened? Did you land on it funny?"

"Yeah, maybe a little," Annabella said. "But it's no big deal, it's not my pitching shoulder. I'll be fine."

Jay-Jay Wright poked his head in. "What happened? Are you okay?"

"Annabella was winning, and Lucas tripped her on purpose," accused Trini.

Lucas's eyes went wide. "Hold up, hold up, that's not what happened! Annabella, you, like, you got your legs messed up with mine because I was ahead, and you were trying to catch up!"

"Listen, Lucas, it's not your fault," Annabella said. "Nobody forced me to race you."

"Yeah, that's true."

Annabella winked. "And the main thing is, I won."

"You did not!"

"It was a tie," said Ben Cutler.

"Yeah, it was a tie!" agreed Lucas.

"Okay, fine," said Annabella.

But she knew the truth.

She was now officially the fastest person in the grade.

CHAPTER EIGHT
TEAMMATES OR RIVALS?

The race at recess ended up being the talk of that night's softball practice, thanks to Sadie Lederman.

"Annabella hurt her shoulder today," Sadie announced while the team stretched out.

"Annabella probably shouldn't pitch for a while," Sadie proclaimed while the team took batting practice.

"Annabella was in a dumb race at recess and fell down hard," Sadie declared while the team ran sprints in the outfield.

"I *won* the race," Annabella said. "Are you going to mention that part?"

Finally, Coach Grandy had had enough. "Both of you, bring it in! The rest of the team, go shag flies."

Annabella and Sadie walked slowly to the dugout, where Coach Grandy was waiting with her hands on her hips.

"Sadie," said the coach. "What are you going on about?"

"Nothing, why?"

"Well, you seem very intent on telling us all about Annabella's day."

Sadie scuffed at the dirt with her toe. "I just think that she does things that she shouldn't do sometimes, especially during the playoffs."

"Sit down, both of you," the coach said.

They did as they were told.

"I don't know what's going on between you two, but I don't like it," said Coach Grandy. "Sadie, no one is more dedicated and passionate about softball than you, and I love that, but sometimes it seems like your head's going to pop off from the pressure you put yourself under. And Annabella, I've told you this before, but you need to make sure we're your number one priority, okay? Between your parties and your school play and your dog walking, it's amazing you have time for softball at all! And what's with running some silly race at school anyway, risking an injury at this point in the season? You could have been seriously hurt!"

"It was Lucas's idea," mumbled Annabella, even though Coach Grandy didn't really want an answer to her question.

"Whatever." The coach clapped her hands together sharply. "Now let's get out there and finish this practice strong. Sadie, you're pitching the next game, and you need to focus on you." She pointed at the mound. "So get out there and do some focusing!"

"Yes, Coach," said Annabella.

"Yes, Coach," said Sadie.

Annabella ran out to shortstop and the rest of the team took their positions as Becky Mertz stepped up to the plate. Becky was the third best hitter on the team after Annabella and Sadie, and she confidently clanked her bat against home plate.

"Batter up!" yelled Coach Grandy.

Sadie wound up and threw a perfect strike. Then she threw two more exactly the same way, with Becky flailing and missing at all of them.

"Jeez, girl, you're on fire," said Becky.

Sadie turned and looked at Annabella. "That's what happens when you don't race boys at recess," she said.

Coach Grandy dropped her head into her hands.

"I knew I should have coached lacrosse," she said.

CHAPTER NINE

ICE CREAM BREAK!

Hey peeps, today we're LIVE at the West Harbor Elementary School auditorium. The first performance of The Lion King is just a week away, and rehearsals are really heating up.

Today's focus is on Trini Tellez, the principal dancer in the cast.

Trini takes the stage . . . the music starts, and it's beautiful . . .

Trini is gliding effortlessly around the stage, bringing us to the Pride Lands of Africa! Look at the height on those jumps!

The music is soaring, and so is Trini . . . this is a tough activity to call folks, there's so much action I can't possibly describe it all but trust me—it's powerful and graceful at the same time.

Now for the big finish . . . Trini leans back at an almost impossible angle and starts spinning faster and faster . . .
but wait, she flips over and lands on her toes, with her arms thrust into the air!
A tremendous finish! She stuck the landing, people! The cast is roaring and cheering, and Mr. Ketchnik is . . .
oh my goodness, I believe he's crying! This could be a first, ladies and gentlemen, the music teacher is crying!

Annabella, who was sitting out the dance part of the rehearsal because of her sore shoulder, watched her friend with her jaw on the floor. She knew her best friend was a dancer, but she had no idea she was a DANCER. The jumps, the twirls, the way she had complete control over every limb, joint, and muscle, how she told a story with her body—it was all just amazing.

When the song ended, Annabella was the first one up on her feet, clapping and cheering.

"That was INCREDIBLE!" yelped Annabella.

Trini beamed at her friend. "Did I remind you of a cheetah?"

"You reminded me of the fastest, strongest cheetah evah!"

After rehearsal, Trini's parents rewarded the two young performers with a trip to the Scooper Dooper Ice Cream Shoppe. As they pulled up, Trini's dad hollered out, "Who wants sundaes?"

Annabella and Trini both hollered, "WE DO!" The Tell-ez's dog, a retriever mix who was named Brownie as a joke because he had a snow-white coat, also said "I DO!" with his eyes and panting mouth.

"Sorry, Brownie, you don't get one," Trini's dad told the dog.

While Trini's parents were inside getting the treats, the girls found seats at a picnic table, where they were quickly spotted by two classmates—twins Charlotte and Charlie Graham. Charlotte played softball with Annabella, and Charlie played Simba in *The Lion King*.

"How's your shoulder?" they both asked Annabella at the same time.

"Are you gonna be able to play in the semifinals?" asked Charlotte.

"Are you gonna be able to prowl around as Scar?" asked Charlie.

Annabella laughed. "Of course I will, and of course I will."

"You're a good actor," Charlie said. "Why do you even play softball?"

"You're a great softball player," Charlotte said. "Why would you want to act in plays?"

"I can't believe you almost beat Lucas in that race, though," Charlie said.

"I can't believe you totally beat Lucas in that race, though," Charlotte said.

"I have a question for you two," Trini said to the twins. "Do you guys know that you always say the same exact thing, but it's also the exact opposite thing?"

"We do," said Charlotte.

"We do not," said Charlie.

"See you guys later!" they both exclaimed.

As they ran off, Trini's parents came back out with the sundaes.

"Do you miss softball at all?" Annabella asked.

Trini had been an excellent softball player herself—in fact, that's how she and Annabella had become such good friends.

"Of course I miss it," Trini answered. "I miss playing with you and all the girls and being part of a team and all that stuff."

"I knew it," Annabella said.

Then Trini added, "But I wouldn't trade what I'm doing for anything in the world. Dance means everything to me. I have so much fun when I'm dancing."

"Wow," Annabella said. "Well, you can sure tell. You're an incredible dancer."

"Thanks," Trini said. "I love it so much."

Annabella looked at her friend. Trini reminded her of Sadie, the way she was so dedicated to one thing. And in a weird way, Trini and Sadie together reminded Annabella of the twins, who were the same but totally opposite. If only there was a way Annabella could help Sadie be more like Trini. That would help Sadie and Annabella get along better *and* help the team!

Her thoughts were interrupted by a question from Trini. "Do you want the rest of my sundae?"

Annabella wasn't sure she heard her friend correctly. "Did you just ask me if I wanted the rest of your sundae?"

"Yup." Trini nodded. "I'm kind of full."

"Wow." Annabella closed her eyes, trying to imagine being unable to finish an ice cream sundae, but after about ten seconds, she gave up.

"So do you want it? Otherwise I'm just going to throw it out."

I probably shouldn't, said Annabella's brain.

"Yes, please!" said her mouth.

CHAPTER TEN

DOGGY DRAMA

Things are hopping at the dog shelter, folks! Over in the Play Yard, Annabella Donatello is in the middle of her favorite game, Race-y Chase-y, with Scruffy, who certainly lives up to his name,

with wild patches of hair sprouting all over the place.

This game is not that complicated, folks: Annabella throws a tennis ball to various corners of the yard,

Scruffy retrieves it, and Annabella chases him around until he gives it back, tail wagging happily.

So, we've been watching all the great things you've been doing recently. Your softball team is now in the semifinals of the league championship, with your great play leading the way. And speaking of play, rehearsals for The Lion King are going well, and I hear you're wowing them as Scar. And perhaps most impressive of all, you just made some very big game-time decisions here at the animal shelter to avoid what could have been an ugly situation. Tell us, Annabella, how do you do it?

Well, to be honest, I take it one game, or one scene, or one dog at a time.

Ha! I love it. Do you ever find it to be too much?

Nah, not really. I mean, it's real busy, and sometimes I might be a little late for a practice or a rehearsal, but *Coach Grandy* and Mr. Ketchnik have been pretty understanding about everything.

THE FREDDY SHOW

Oh, that's great. Is it fun being so busy?
Totally! My mom calls me the Everything Girl because I'm lucky enough to be able to do a bunch of different things, and I wouldn't have it any other way.
Well, thanks very much, Annabella. We've taken up too much time from your very full schedule already!
Oh, no problem! Gotta go to practice! Bye!

CHAPTER ELEVEN

A DISAPPOINTING WIN

Then came the game that changed everything.

It's the semifinals of the league playoffs, folks! The West Harbor Smashers have been looking really good, winning the previous game 6–1 thanks to the pitching of Annabella Donatello and the hitting of pretty much everyone!

Today, however, with Annabella resting her arm, Sadie Lederman will be pitching . . .

she's had an up-and-down season on the hill this year, and it will be interesting to see how today goes . . .

Things only got worse from there.

The next three batters all got hits, and just like that, Ridgeville was ahead 3–0. Sadie looked like she wanted to crawl beneath the mound.

Coach Grandy hustled out to talk to her.

"Relax!" she said. "You got this! Just stop pressing so much!"

Sadie nodded unconvincingly.

Her next pitch was about three feet outside.

"Outside," said the umpire, unnecessarily.

Sadie's next pitch was so inside it almost hit the batter, who went sprawling in the dirt to get out of the way.

"Are you trying to kill my third baseman?" hollered the Ridgeville coach.

Annabella jogged in from shortstop. "Everything okay?"

Sadie glared at Annabella. "Oh, so now you're being all nice?"

"I'm making sure you're good. Try to pretend it's practice and we're just fooling around—"

"Wait, you're saying I can't pitch in games? I'm only good in practice?"

"No, of course not! I'm not saying that at all! Stop being so weird!"

"I'm not being weird!"

"Yes, you are!"

Coach Grandy shot out of the dugout with her hands on her hips. "GIRLS, ENOUGH!"

Annabella ran back to her position. Sadie took a deep breath, peered in toward the batter, wound up, and threw.

The pitch bounced twice before it reached home plate.

Sadie looked like she was about to cry. "You know what? I don't even want to pitch!" She flung her mitt, which happened to be her most accurate throw of the day—it went right over the plate. "I STINK!"

Coach Grandy ran to the mound and took out her temperamental pitcher, but things didn't get much better from there. Three more pitchers—Ellen Greenfield, Kellyanne Baptiste, and Isa Shulman—gave up nine more runs. But the good news was, the West Harbor bats were on fire, and behind three hits each from Annabella, Becky Mertz, and Charlotte Graham, they ended up winning the game 14–12.

Sadie Lederman spent the rest of the game on the bench.

And that's it, folks—it was a total slugfest, but West Harbor survives, and they'll meet the Dixville Dingers for the league championship! That game promises to be a humdinger!!

See what I did there? With the double dinger? I know, I know . . . I'm good.

We're the Bashers!

We're the—

But Coach Grandy held up her hand and interrupted the chant. "I don't really think this is cause for celebration," she said. "We won, yes, but I'm extremely disappointed with some of the things that went on today. Our behavior was less than perfect. We don't argue with one another, and we certainly don't sulk or quit if things aren't going our way."

No one said anything, but everyone knew what—and who—Coach Grandy was talking about. Sadie Lederman was still sitting by herself on the bench, in the same spot she'd spent most of the game.

"We need to fix this before the championship game," said Coach Grandy. "As a result, we are going to have one last practice, at six p.m. the night before the game. Attendance will be mandatory, with absolutely no exceptions. It's essential that we learn how to be a team again, to play for each other, and to come together as a family."

After Coach Grandy finished speaking, Annabella walked to the opposite side of the bench as Sadie and sat down. Annabella felt a strange thump in her heart, and her blood suddenly turned hot as it raced through her body.

Mandatory. No exceptions.

The practice was Friday night.

The same night as the first performance of *The Lion King.*

CHAPTER TWELVE
ANNABELLA'S DILEMMA

On the car ride home, Annabella explained the whole thing to her mom: Sadie's terrible pitching, their argument on the mound, Sadie throwing her glove, Coach Grandy getting upset and then announcing the mandatory, no-exceptions practice.

"Well, at least you won the game," said Ms. Donatello.

"Yeah, but Mom, what am I going to do? Opening night of *The Lion King* and the practice are on the same night!"

"Um, skip them both so you can rest up for Park 'n' Bark the next day?"

"Ha! Very funny, Ma. You know I'm coming to that, right? I'll be there as soon as I can, right after the game."

"Of course, honey! I'm just sorry I have to miss the game."

Annabella sighed sadly. "Not as sorry as I am to miss most of Park 'n' Bark."

The annual Park 'n' Bark was Annabella's favorite adoption event. Once a year, the shelter would bring in a giant trailer full of pets needing homes, and people came from miles around to find their dream animal. Annabella got so happy thinking about it that she forgot about her problem for five seconds.

But in the sixth second, she fell back against her seat in frustration. "MOM!" she wailed. "What am I going to do?"

Ms. Donatello glanced over at her daughter. "Annabean, remember what we talked about a few weeks ago? This is what I was worried about. The only thing I'll say is that you're just a kid, and these aren't exactly life-and-death decisions. And the opening night of a show is very different from a softball practice."

"Yup, I agree." Annabella thought for a minute. "I mean,

Coach Grandy has been pretty nice and understanding about everything so far, so it's not going to be a big deal if I can't make one practice, right?"

"Right," said Annabella's mom, even though something inside was telling her, *Wrong.*

⚾ ⚾ ⚾

After having dinner, dessert, and the little extra dessert she snuck when her mom wasn't looking, Annabella took a deep breath and picked up the phone.

"Hello, this is Jennifer Grandy."

"Hi, Coach Grandy! How are you doing? It's Annabella."

"Well, my goodness, Annabella. Please don't tell me you have a sore arm!"

"Hahahahaha!" chirped Annabella, over-laughing. "Oh no, Coach Grandy. Definitely not. Yeah, no, but, uh, I am calling because I needed to talk about Friday night."

"Oh good, I wanted to talk about that with you too. Before we start practice, I'd like for you and Sadie to address the team together, like a pep talk, so your teammates can see that you've put your differences behind you."

"Well, uh . . . well, the thing is, it's just that, well, it turns out I can't make the practice because I have the first performance of my school play that night."

"The school play?"

"Yes. I'm playing Scar in *The Lion King*."

"Oh, right. The mean lion."

"Yes, and it's opening night, which means it's the first—"

"I know what an opening night is."

"Oh, okay, great, well, since it's our opening night, you know, that's why it's really important."

"I see." Coach Grandy paused for about five seconds, which to Annabella felt like five years. "Well, don't you think bringing our team together on the night before the championship is also really important?"

"Oh, uh, yes, sure."

"And do you believe in the concept of a team?"

"Of course I do."

"And have you thought about what it means to be a good teammate?"

"I, uh—"

"Annabella, a teammate doesn't abandon other teammates at the most important moment of the season. That would *not* be good. In fact, those teammates might not want to welcome that teammate back onto their team next year, and I can't say I would blame them."

Annabella breathed into the phone, trying to figure out what Coach Grandy meant. Was she saying that if Annabella missed practice, she wouldn't be allowed on the team next year? That would be horrible! Annabella loved softball!

"I love softball!" Annabella said out loud. "I would hate not being on the team next year!"

"You have told me several times how much you love softball, but sometimes I'm not so sure," said the coach. "Do you remember several months ago when you missed batting practice because you had to get a present for your friend before a birthday party? And then, when you told me you were auditioning for this play, you made a promise to me that it would not in any way distract you from your responsibilities to the team. I think I have been very patient with your busy schedule. But my patience is beginning to wear thin."

"I know my responsibilities to the team, I swear!"

Annabella could hear Coach Grandy sigh through the phone. "Is there anyone else who can play the part of Scar?"

"I mean, there's an understudy, which means a person who would do it if I were sick, but he's still learning the lines—"

"Well, think of what a wonderful opportunity this will be for that young performer. And then you can return for the rest of the performances."

Annabella couldn't quite believe what she was hearing. A tear formed in her right eye, which she quickly wiped away.

"Yes, Coach Grandy. I understand. I will be at practice."

Coach Grandy sighed again, but this time it was a much more satisfied sigh. "Good. I'll see you at practice."

After the call ended, Annabella just sat there, frozen.

"All good?" asked her mom.

"I guess," said Annabella, not exactly answering the question.

When Annabella finally put the phone down, she did the math in her head.

Two events, two places to be, and one incredible mess.

CHAPTER THIRTEEN
CRASHING THE MEETING

At lunch the next day, Annabella called an emergency meeting with Trini Tellez, Ben Cutler, and Jay-Jay Wright, where she explained the whole situation. Lucas McGoish was at the next table over, balancing French fries on his nose while his pals Matty and Andre cheered him on.

"So I'm supposed to miss opening night of the play," Annabella told her friends. "All because of a softball practice that we're only having because Sadie Lederman threw a temper tantrum."

"That's so unfair," said Trini.

"Absolutely ridiculous," said Jay-Jay.

"What a joke," said Ben.

Annabella eyed her friends. "You guys are NOT being helpful."

"Okay, sorry," Trini said. "So, like, is there anything you can do? Like, can you figure out a way to skip it? Come up with some excuse?"

"You could say your car broke down!" Ben suggested.

"You could say you overslept!" Jay-Jay offered.

"You could say your understudy got the measles!" Trini proposed.

But Annabella shook her head every time. "Yeah, those are some of the worst ideas I've ever heard," she said. "But thanks."

Lucas McGoish, who had been listening the whole time, couldn't take it anymore and walked over to their table.

"Dudes," he said, barging into the conversation. "What is UP?"

"This doesn't concern you," said Trini, which was Lucas's cue to grab a chair and sit down.

"What time is the practice?" he asked Annabella.

"Six to eight."

"And what time is the play?"

"Seven thirty, but I have to be there by six forty-five."

Lucas stretched his back with a loud *CRACK!*

"In that case," he said, "you've got it all wrong."

"We've got *what* all wrong?" asked Jay-Jay.

"All of it," Lucas said. "You've got all of it all wrong."

Annabella rolled her eyes. "Is that so, Mr. Expert on Everything? Well, please save the day for us."

"Glad to." Lucas grabbed one of Trini's fish sticks.

"Sure, help yourself," Trini said, well after the fact.

"Here's the thing," Lucas said, with his mouth full. "These coaches, they talk a big game. They say they want full dedication and full commitment, and they throw a conniption if you show any interest in anything else. But the truth is, they'll take what they can get. Especially with the superstars like Annabella. If you gave your softball coach, like, a truth syrup, and asked her, 'Annabella can't stay for the whole practice. Are you really going to kick her off the team if she leaves early?' I guarantee you she would say, 'Absolutely not! She's my best player!'"

"Wait a second," said Jay-Jay. "So then she should tell her coach that she can go to practice but has to leave after, like, twenty minutes?"

"Oh, absolutely not," said Lucas. "You have to make something up."

And with that, Lucas got up and walked back to his table. Annabella stared at him, trying to decide if she was annoyed at his rude interruption, pleased that he'd called her a superstar, or shocked at the fact that what he'd said actually made a lot of sense.

ANNOYED

SHOCKED

PLEASED

"It's actually truth *serum*," Trini told Lucas.

"Whatever," Lucas said, chomping on a piece of red licorice.

"Hey, Ben," Annabella said. "Remember your championship game against Jogo Bonito last year, when your dog barged onto the field and just, like, practically ruined everything, but then it turned out to be the most hilarious thing in the world and everyone thought it was totally awesome?"

"Yeah, of course," Ben said. "Why?"

Annabella started twirling the ends of her hair, which is something she did when she was deep in thought.

"I have an idea," she told her friends.

Approximately four and a half minutes later, that idea was a full-fledged plan.

CHAPTER FOURTEEN

A BUSY NIGHT, PART I

> Busy night tonight, folks! We've got the West Harbor Bashers holding their last practice of the year down at Woodlands Park, and then a few miles away, opening night of *The Lion King*! And we've got one young lady, Annabella Donatello, who's scheduled to play leading roles at both events . . . Can you feel the excitement tonight?!?!?!

After about fifteen minutes of the team stretching and playing catch, Coach Grandy blew her whistle with a loud *TWEEEET*!

"Bring it in! Everybody at home plate!" she hollered. "Team meeting. Leave your bats and gloves in the dugout."

The girls gathered in a circle, murmuring to each other.

"What's going on?" Annabella whispered to Becky Mertz.

"I have no idea," said Becky. "All I know is that team meetings make me nervous."

Coach Grandy held up her hand and the murmuring stopped.

"I want to start this practice a little differently," said the coach. Annabella noticed the coach was looking right at her. "We all need to remember something: As important as it is to play together as a team on the field, it's just as important to come together as a team off the field. So, to start off, I would like to do a short exercise. Everyone is going to pair off with a teammate, and you'll each tell the other what you most admire and appreciate about them. Sadie and Annabella, you two go first."

Annabella blinked twice as a nervous buzz flashed through her body. The last thing she wanted right now was to be the center of attention. But everyone was staring at her, so she and Sadie moved to the middle of the circle.

"Annabella, you start," said the coach.

"Uh, okay." She looked at her teammate, who was staring at her expectantly. "Well, Sadie, I really admire and appreciate the way you put everything you have into the game of softball. You're so dedicated, and you work so hard, and you've become a really great player, and everyone knows it. So . . . uh, yeah, so that's what I really admire and appreciate about you." Sadie looked slightly disappointed, so Annabella added, "And you're a nice person."

"Great!" Coach Grandy turned to Sadie. "Your turn."

Sadie took a deep breath. "Okay, right, yeah. Annabella, I admire and appreciate your attit—"

But that was as far as she got, because right then Selma Menzo yelled, "Look! A dog!"

"Well, that was impressive, Annabella," said Coach Grandy.

"I bet I know what happened!" Annabella exclaimed. "There's a big adoption event at my mom's shelter tomorrow. They're bringing in lots of dogs to get adopted, and this dog must have escaped! I need to bring her back!"

"Are you sure?"

"Yeah! It's really close, I can walk there."

Coach Grandy frowned. "Fine, but I expect you back here right after."

"I'll try for sure!"

This is fascinating, folks! Annabella Donatello has left practice to help the lost dog get back to the shelter. Coach Grandy is watching her star player leave, a look of confusion on her face . . .

But when Annabella took the stray dog out to the parking lot, she did not walk west toward the shelter. She also did not walk east toward her house or south toward the Scooper Dooper Ice Cream Shoppe for a sundae. Instead, she walked north for five minutes until she got to Trini Tellez's house.

Annabella handed the dog to Trini, and Trini handed a shopping bag to Annabella.

"Jeez," said Trini, "you cut it close, I was getting worried! Everything work out okay?"

"Better than okay!" said Annabella.

"Great! But we need to go."

When Trini's dad dropped them off at the high school, Annabella's mom was just getting out of her car. "How was Trini's?" she asked her daughter. "Did you have a nice time warming up at her house?"

"Oh, uh, yup," Annabella said, not looking her mother in the eye.

Inside the school, Annabella found a bathroom, opened the shopping bag, pulled out her costume, put it on, sprinted down the hall toward the auditorium, and immediately ran into Mr. Ketchnik.

"Scar the star!" he proclaimed. "The excitement is building!" Then he frowned. "You're a few minutes late. Why is your face so red? Why are you out of breath?"

"Uh, well, I forgot part of my costume at home and had to run back and get it."

"Oh my word! Which part?"

"Uh . . . the whiskers."

Mr. Ketchnik whistled. "Well, we can't have a lion without her whiskers now, can we?" He patted Annabella on the shoulder. "Have a great show, my dear."

"I sure will!"

Annabella ran into the makeup room thinking about how she had just lied to two people in two minutes.

She shook her head. She had to forget about it.

She had a show to do.

CHAPTER FIFTEEN

A BUSY NIGHT, PART II

I can honestly say this has been one of the most impressive performances of *The Lion King* I've ever seen, and that includes ALL the movie adaptations! The acting, the singing, the dancing, the thrills, the suspense, the danger . . . it's incredibly exciting. Oooh, and here comes the big scene where Scar threatens Simba . . .

Annabella went into her crouch. Charlie Graham, as Simba, looked up at her in fear.

"Why are you doing this?" said Charlie/Simba.

Annabella/Scar glowered and stalked. "Life's not fair, is it? You see, I shall never be king. And you shall never see the light of another day."

Offstage, Mr. Ketchnik pushed a button, and a huge roar of thunder blasted from the speakers. The crowd gasped, both because of the sound and because all of a sudden, one of the larger branches on the paper-mache tree onstage split and dangled dangerously over poor Simba's head.

"Uh-oh," Annabella said.

That was not part of the script.

"Uh-oh?" Charlie asked. "Uh-oh what?"

"Uh-oh that," she said, and pointed up just as the branch fully broke away and started tumbling through the air.

"DUCK!" yelled Annabella.

Ladies and gentlemen, I do not believe this is part of the show! The director, Mr. Ketchnik, is running down the aisle toward the stage, waving his arms, but he's not going to get there in time . . .

the branch is gaining speed . . . but WAIT! Scar, otherwise known as Annabella Donatello, grabs one of the prop coconuts off the ground and flings it at the branch . . . and it's a direct hit!

The coconut knocks the branch out of harm's way just before it clonks poor Simba on the head! Wow, what an incredibly athletic play by this young performer!

When the show ended, the audience stood and cheered, and backstage, everyone congratulated Annabella for both her splendid performance and her heroic, quick-thinking actions.

"THIS is why it's so important to get athletes interested in the performing arts!" crowed Mr. Ketchnik.

Annabella's mom gave her a big hug. "You were incredible, honey!"

Trini's parents hugged their daughter, then their daughter's best friend.

"You guys were just incredible," said Mr. Tellez. "This calls for double hot fudge sundaes, if you ask me."

"I agree!" said Ms. Donatello.

Trini looked at Annabella. "Whaddya say, Scar?"

Annabella gave her best smile. "I'd love to," she said. "But you know what? I'm actually really tired, and I have the game tomorrow, and then the Park 'n' Bark adoption event, and then another performance at night. I think I'll just go home and take it easy."

Trini looked at her like she'd just grown another head. "Saying no to ice cream? Who are you, and what have you done with my best friend?"

Annabella tried to laugh. "I know, right?"

The plan had worked—she'd made it to practice, and to the show, saved her costar from getting bonked on the head, and gotten a standing ovation!

Everything had worked out just right!

So why did Annabella feel a tiny bit wrong?

CHAPTER SIXTEEN

THE BIG GAME

This has been a championship game for the ages . . .
what a battle! Annabella Donatello has been
her usual dominant self on the mound, giving up
only a single run on three hits.

But the Dixville pitcher has been equally effective,
also giving up only one run, on an RBI single by Becky Mertz.
So we're going to extra innings,

and Annabella is going to have
to come out of the game, since
no one is allowed to pitch
more than six innings . . .

In the dugout, Coach Grandy had a decision to make.

Her ace had pitched brilliantly, but now the coach had to put in someone else.

As she stood at one end of the dugout, trying to figure out what to do, there was a shuffling of feet beside her.

"Uh, Coach Grandy?"

The coach looked up. "What is it, Annabella? I don't really have time to—"

"I think you should put Sadie in to pitch."

Coach Grandy sighed. "You do? And why is that? Especially after what happened last time?"

Annabella took a deep, nervous breath. "I don't . . . I don't know, I guess I just think she deserves this opportunity. She's worked so hard." She paused before adding, "Like my mom said, it's not life-or-death. But it might really crush her if she doesn't get to make up for her mistake."

Coach Grandy peered down at her star player and her eyes softened. "You're a pretty smart kid, you know that?"

It looks like Sadie Lederman is taking the mound here in the top of the seventh inning . . .

This is a bit of a surprise, considering what happened the last time she pitched . . . but everyone loves a comeback story, am I right?

She looks in at the first batter . . . here comes the wind-up . . . and

OH NO!
SHE HITS THE BATTER!
Right in the shoulder!
The batter appears to be just fine as she jogs down to first base . . .

Annabella watched Coach Grandy pace in the dug-out, and it looked like she might decide to take Sadie out already.

"Time out!" yelled Annabella. "Time out!"

She hurried over to her teammate, who was kicking the dirt with her cleats. "Hey!" she said brightly, trying to sound upbeat. "Come on, Sadie, you can do this!"

Sadie didn't even look at her. "Yeah, sure. Here we go again, right? Worst pitcher EVER!"

"Stop it!" Annabella said forcefully. "You got this! You're a great player, you just need to stop taking everything so seriously! If we win, that's great, but if we lose, that's okay too, we'll get 'em next time!"

"But it's the last game," Sadie said quietly. "There is no next time."

Annabella grinned. "Then we'll get 'em next season, after we have an awesome summer goofing around and forgetting all about it!"

The umpire came out to the mound. "Okay, you two, coffee break is over. Let's play ball!"

Annabella looked at her teammate. "Have fun! You got this." Then she winked. "I admire and appreciate you."

Which is when Sadie did something she'd never done on a softball field before.

She giggled.

Wow, I don't know what happened in that little conference at the mound, but Sadie Lederman blew the next three batters away, with two strikeouts and a weak grounder to second base.

She's getting high fives from all her teammates as they go back into the dugout, but they're still behind . . . West Harbor comes to bat here in the bottom of the seventh down by a run . . .

The new pitcher for Dixville was a tall girl with very long arms that practically reached home plate by the time she released the ball. The first two batters for West Harbor, Kristen Rathbun and Aaliytha Stephens, struck out swinging.

"Jeez, where've they been hiding her?" muttered Coach Grandy in the dugout.

West Harbor was down to their last out. Next up was Charlotte Graham. She swung and missed at the first pitch, but then watched two balls go by, fouled off three pitches, watched another ball, hit two more foul balls, then finally worked out a walk.

The girls cheered mightily from the dugout.

"Here we go!" yelled Annabella. Then she realized she was on deck and grabbed her bat and helmet. She called out to Sadie, who was stepping into the batter's box.

"Summer goofing off, here we come!"

Sadie Lederman steps into the batter's box . . .

here comes the pitch . . .

and she laces it right up the middle for a base hit!

"YES!" yelled Annabella, when Sadie got her hit. Now it was her turn. She stepped into the batter's box and pounded her bat on the plate.

The pitcher wound up and threw . . . and suddenly, Annabella felt paralyzed.

The ball whizzed by her.

"STRIKE ONE!"

Annabella stepped out of the batter's box, trying to calm down, but her mind was racing.

What was going on? What was she feeling?

Was it disappointment because her mom couldn't be there, since she was at the Park 'n' Bark? Was it nerves because the league championship was on the line? Or was it guilt about what she'd had to do the day before, when she'd lied twice to make sure she could be in the show without Coach Grandy cutting her from the team?

"Batter up!" said the umpire.

Annabella stepped back in, but thoughts were still racing through her mind as the long-limbed pitcher wound up and threw.

Swing and a miss.

"STRIKE TWO!"

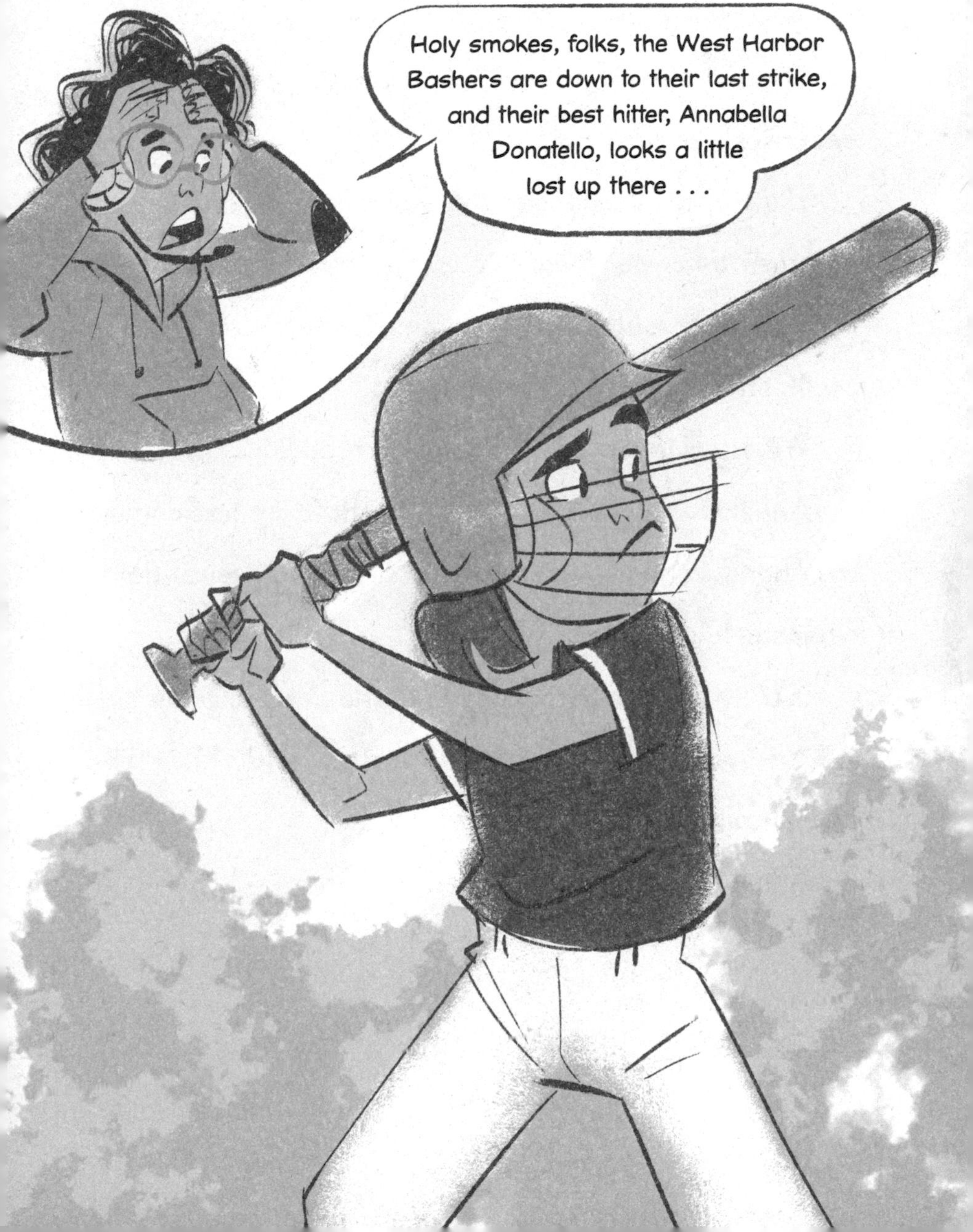

Annabella needed to calm down and get herself right. She stepped out of the batter's box again, trying to figure out what to do.

Then she remembered: Mr. Ketchnik's breathing exercises!

Think of the ocean, and the waves going in and out . . . and then time your breathing to the waves you see in your mind . . . in . . . out . . . in . . . out . . .

"Come on young lady, batter up!"

Waves going in . . . waves going out . . .

Annabella felt herself relax . . . with a calmness coming over her . . . and a joy in remembering that she was doing what she loved . . .

It truly was the perfect day . . . the perfect game . . .

And when the pitcher wound up and threw the perfect pitch?

Annabella was ready for it.

No! It hits the wall!

The left fielder gives chase . . .
Becky Mertz is flying around
the bases, she scores easily . . .
Here comes Sadie Lederman,
past second and heading for third . . .

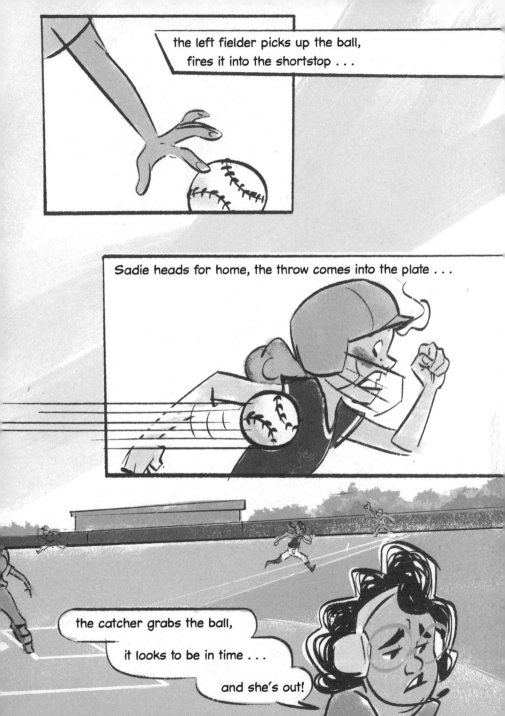

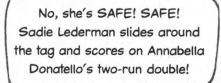

No, she's SAFE! SAFE! Sadie Lederman slides around the tag and scores on Annabella Donatello's two-run double!

THE WEST HARBOR BASHERS WIN 3–2!

THEY'RE STATE CHAMPS!!!!!

Sadie was swarmed by half the team, Annabella was swarmed by the other half, and then they found each other, the two best players on the team, united in victory.

"I NEVER GOT TO TELL YOU AT PRACTICE YESTERDAY WHAT I ADMIRE AND APPRECIATE ABOUT YOU!" Sadie yelled over the cheers of her teammates. "YOU'RE A SUPPORTIVE PERSON WHO LOVES LIFE, AND I WISH I WAS MORE LIKE YOU!"

"THAT'S SO NICE!" Annabella yelled back. "BUT YOU DON'T NEED TO BE MORE LIKE ME! YOU CAN JUST BE MORE LIKE YOU!"

Then they laughed and hugged and agreed that it was turning out to be a perfect day.

CHAPTER SEVENTEEN
CAUGHT!

The rest of the day, however, turned out to be not quite as perfect.

In fact, it was kind of the opposite of perfect.

After the celebrating and the hugs and the snacks and the parents' gift to Coach Grandy, Annabella told her coach and teammates that she had to go. "I need to get down to my mom's shelter for the Park 'n' Bark event before it closes," she said.

"Wow, you really do love dogs," Coach Grandy said. "Almost as much as softball, I bet!"

"Just as much," Annabella said. "Maybe even more."

The coach laughed. "You're quite the character, Annabella Donatello," she said. "Go on, get out of here."

Annabella ran to the hill behind the outfield, where she met Trini, Jay-Jay, and Ben. The first thing Annabella did was bend down and give Trini's dog a hug.

"You nailed it last night, Brownie," she said. "A whole bag of extra treats for you!"

As they walked downtown to the West Harbor Animal Rescue Center, the four friends went over the events of the last two days. They talked about Annabella leaving practice early to "rescue" a dog, and opening night, and about how she threw a coconut at the falling tree branch to save Charlie, and how she got herself to relax and get the winning hit in the game.

"The plan worked perfectly!" said Jay-Jay.

"You really fooled them!" said Ben.

"The master of deception!" said Trini.

For some reason, all these compliments weren't exactly making Annabella feel great.

By the time they turned the corner to the shelter, the adoption event was winding down. There were only a few cars left in the parking lot and even fewer dogs in cages outside the giant trailer.

The first thing Annabella did was look for someone she hoped not to find . . .

But Scruffy was still there. And still not adopted.

"Hey, Scruff," she said, bending down to give him a scratch. He licked her hand, happy to see her, but Annabella thought his eyes seemed a little sad. *Dogs understand a lot more than people realize*, she thought.

Annabella's mom ran over and gave her a hug. "You made it!" she exclaimed. "Congrats, league champions!! I got a text from Selma's mom about the game! Sounds incredible!"

"Annabella had the game-winning hit," Trini announced.

"Wow! Incredible!" Ms. Donatello said, beaming. "And we got twenty-two dogs and sixteen cats adopted, so it was a great day all around!"

"Amazing!" said Annabella. Nothing made her happier than animals finding homes. "Can we take Scruffy out to play? Maybe Brownie can cheer him up."

"Go for it!" said her mom.

Sure enough, after a few sniffs and circles, Scruffy and Brownie decided to be best friends, and they tore around the yard in a game of Race-y Chase-y. Other dogs joined in, and soon Annabella and her pals were in the middle of a doggy free-for-all.

Then Jay-Jay pointed toward the parking lot. "Hey, isn't that the softball coach?"

"And, uh, isn't that pretty much the whole team behind her?" Ben added.

Annabella turned to look, and her heart immediately started thumping wildly. Sure enough, there was Coach Grandy and about ten of Annabella's softball teammates heading right toward them.

"Hello, everyone!" Coach Grandy said. "We were celebrating our great win, and a bunch of us decided to come over and see how the big adoption event was coming along."

"That's so nice!" exclaimed Ms. Donatello. "We had a great day, just like the Smashers! Can I interest you in a dog or cat? We have several left!"

It didn't take long for Coach Grandy to spot Brownie. "I see that little rascal is still here. I guess no one wanted to adopt her after her great escape last night?"

Ms. Donatello cocked her head in confusion. "I'm sorry, which dog are you talking about? And what great escape?"

Coach Grandy pointed at Brownie. "That one. The white one."

Annabella's mom laughed. "Brownie? Oh, she's not available. That's Annabella's friend Trini's dog. Isn't she adorable?"

That was the moment Annabella's heart fell completely out of her chest.

Coach Grandy swiveled her head over to her star player. "Annabella? What's happening here? Last night at practice you said this dog was a runaway from the shelter."

So close, Annabella thought. *I was so close to a clean getaway.*

"I—uh—"

"You said you had to bring her back here," Coach Grandy said. "Which is why you had to leave practice early."

Annabella watched her mom's face go through a bunch of expressions—surprise, confusion, disappointment.

"Ah, I see," Ms. Donatello said. She looked at her daughter, but Annabella was not quite able to speak.

"You were very convincing, Annabella," Coach Grandy said. "I guess all that acting practice really paid off."

Annabella laughed nervously, but no one else did.

"I . . . I . . ." Annabella was trying to form the right words—any words, actually—to explain what happened and what she had done.

Sadie Lederman went up to her new favorite teammate. "Annabella, is everything okay?"

"Well . . . uh . . ." Annabella's eyes swept across every-one—her mom, Coach Grandy, Sadie, her friends Trini, Ben, and Jay-Jay, the rest of her teammates, even the strangers who wanted to adopt an animal—and realized that the only thing to do was to tell the truth about why she hadn't told the truth.

"I lied," Annabella said. "I lied, and I'm really sorry. It's true, this is Brownie, my friend Trini's dog. I made up the whole story last night about her running away from the shelter so I could leave practice early and get to opening night of my show on time. I am really sorry about that." Then she hesitated before adding, "But I don't regret it."

"Honey?" said Annabella's mom. "Really?"

"Really I lied, or really I don't regret it?"

"Both, I guess."

Annabella walked over to her coach. "I love softball, Coach Grandy, I really do, but I love performing too. I know you said my understudy could do it, but I had worked really hard, and those cast members are my teammates too. It didn't seem fair that I would maybe get cut from the softball team next year just for missing a practice. So I came up with the plan, and I lied."

Everyone looked at Coach Grandy, who looked like she was about to say something but then decided not to. Instead, she just looked at the ground.

Annabella walked over to her mother and took her hand. "I wish I didn't have to lie, Ma, but I didn't feel like I had any other choice."

Then Annabella sat down between Brownie and Scruffy and started petting them both.

No one moved or said anything for a few seconds until Annabella's mom bent down and sat next to her daughter. "I wish I had more time to watch you do all the things you love—softball, and acting, and soccer, and drawing, and flying kites! But what I do know is that you should keep doing it. Keep doing it all, and do it however you want, whenever you want, wherever you want. That's up to you, and no one else."

Annabella hugged her mother. "Thank you, Mom."

"I love you, Annabean."

Coach Grandy cleared her throat. "I also want to say something. Annabella, I put you in that position. I let my emotions get the better of me, and I insisted that you come to practice, and I threatened to not include you on the team next season. I convinced myself I was doing those things to help the team, but I realize that I really did them because I put winning above everything. That was wrong, and I'm very sorry."

Annabella felt a comforting warmth spread through-out her body. "Thank you so much for saying that." Then she slapped her forehead with her hand. "Oh, wait! I was thinking about something else, too. The breathing exercises I learned from Mr. Ketchnik helped me get that big hit today! And the pitching technique I learned from Coach Grandy helped me save Charlie from getting hit by that branch at the performance last night! So it turns out to be really helpful that I do lots of different things. Right?"

"One hundred percent," said Coach Grandy.

"Yay!" Annabella said. "I knew it!"

Trini Tellez raised her hand. "Just to remind everyone, there are some dogs and cats here who need homes, in case anyone is interested."

Right then Sadie picked up an old, tattered Frisbee and threw it across the yard.

"Fetch!" she yelled.

Five dogs gave chase, and Sadie, Trini, Ben, and Jay-Jay ran after them. The rest of the team followed, and soon the yard was full of yelling, barking, laughing, and joyous sounds of play.

"That's what I like to hear," said Annabella's mom.

Coach Grandy stepped forward shyly. "Actually, I do think I would like to adopt a dog," she said.

"Really?" asked Annabella.

"Really," answered her coach.

Annabella immediately ran out to the yard and retrieved Scruffy. "This is Scruffy, the greatest dog ever," Annabella said.

Coach Grandy bent down to say hello, and the dog gave her a big lick right across her nose.

The no-nonsense coach burst out in a giant smile.

"Scruffy Grandy," she said. "It has a pretty nice ring to it!"

CHAPTER EIGHTEEN
ALL STORIES SHOULD END WITH ICE CREAM

That night's performance of *The Lion King* went beautifully—the acting was moving, the singing was glorious, the dancing was magnificent, and not a single branch fell from a single tree.

At the end of the show, the first person to stand and cheer was Sadie Lederman.

"BRAVO!!" she yelled. "BRAVO!"

In the hallway, when the actors came out, Sadie rushed up to Annabella and Trini.

"I'm going to try out for the school play next year!" she announced. Then she started singing at the top of her lungs. *"Can you feel the love tonight?"*

Annabella and Trini looked at each other. They were both thinking the same thing.

Sadie is not the greatest singer in the world. In fact, she's kind of terrible.

"We would love to have you!" said Trini.

"It's going to be so much fun!" said Annabella.

"I can't wait!" said Sadie.

"YAY!" they all squealed.

The three girls hugged and went outside into the cool spring night air.

Next stop? Ice cream.

It was a perfect night . . . a perfect show . . . and so what if Sadie doesn't have the perfect singing voice? If she wants to be in the show next year, then good for her!!

NOW'S YOUR CHANTS!

Team chants are awesome!

They're great for team spirit and the perfect opportunity to make up a silly song that rhymes.

The Smashers had it pretty easy, because they had a lot of words to rhyme with. They used Bashers, Slashers, and Mashers but could've used a few more if they wanted to, like Crashers, Dashers, and Thrashers.

But what if your team name was a little trickier?

Okay, so try this. You just found out you've been selected to write the team chant, and you have to turn it in by the next practice. And you're really excited—until you remember what the team name is.

The Armadillos.

Uh-oh!

Can you do it?

Can you write the Armadillo team chant?

Give it a try in the space below!

Ready . . . GO!

_____

_____

_____

_____

_____

_____

_____

_____

_____

GOOD NAMES
FOR BAD GUYS

Why is it that a lot of times, bad guys have the most fun?

They're the ones you love to hate. The ones that aren't just evil, but *entertainingly* evil.

And they have the best names! Scar, the bad guy in *The Lion King*, has a great name. *SCAR*. Yikes . . . just saying it out loud gives you the shivers. A few more great bad guy names are Cruella de Vil, Miss Trunchbull, and of course, VOLDEMORT.

Can you dream up some fun names for bad guys? Here are a few to get you started:

Grimsby   _____

Peter Pain   _____

Madame Misery   _____

The Ouchster   _____

Disastro

_____

WHAT IS YOUR PERFECT DAY?

For some people, it's doing one thing.

For other people, it's doing two things.

And for still other people, it's doing lots and lots and lots of things.

There's no right or wrong way to spend a day as long as you're doing what you love and not hurting anyone along the way. Sure, you might have to throw in a little homework or yardwork, but that's part of the deal, right? And it's probably not the *best* idea to spend all your free time staring at a screen, because even that can get boring. But finding things you like to do and doing them with friends or teammates or bandmates or fellow cast members, or by yourself—that sounds just about PERFECT.

So how about it? What's your idea of a perfect day? Please use the space below to list all the great things you would do.

There is only one ground rule to this exercise:

You're only allowed to put "eating ice cream" once.

_____

_____

_____

_____

_____

_____

_____

_____

_____

_____

_____

ACKNOWLEDGMENTS

A shout-out to the usual, invaluable help from Erica, Amy, Lesley, Megan, Rachael, Brann, and Micah, and especially to you, the readers, for honoring me by reading these stories! Writing books is a privilege that I never take for granted, and it's all thanks to you!

ABOUT THE AUTHOR

Tommy Greenwald is the author of *Game Changer*, *Rivals*, and *Dinged*. *Game Changer* is on nineteen state lists, was an Amazon Best Book of the Month, a YALSA Top Ten pick, and a Junior Library Guild Premier selection. *Rivals* was also an Amazon Best Book of the Month, a Junior Library Guild selection, and a YALSA Quick Pick for Reluctant Young Adult Readers. Greenwald is also the author of the Crimebiters! and Charlie Joe Jackson series, among many other books for children. To read woefully outdated information about him, visit tommygreenwald.com.

ABOUT THE ILLUSTRATOR

Lesley Vamos earned a bachelor's in digital media with high distinction from the University of New South Wales Art and Design, along with an honorary award in hand-drawn animation despite continuing to hold her pencil incorrectly. Lesley has been running her illustration and design business for over a decade and is passionate about telling stories that put good into the world. She lives in Sydney, Australia, with her partner, two littles, and small floofer, Penny.